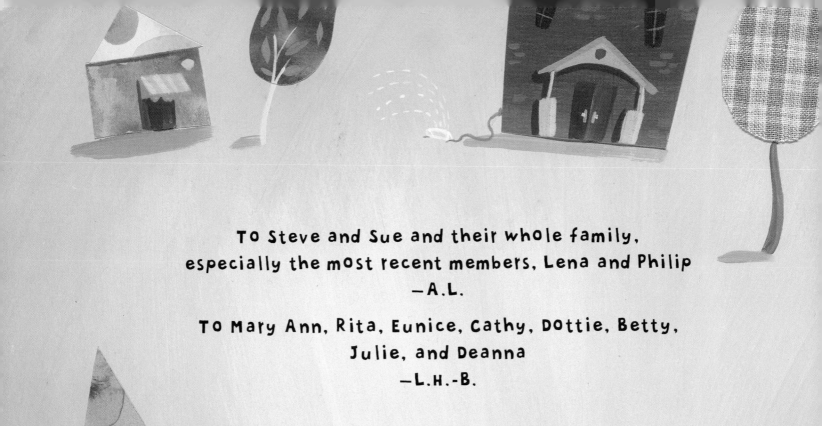

TO Steve and Sue and their whole family,
especially the most recent members, Lena and Philip
—A.L.

TO Mary Ann, Rita, Eunice, Cathy, Dottie, Betty,
Julie, and Deanna
—L.H.-B.

Aunt Lucy Went to Buy a Hat
Text copyright © 2004 by Alice Low
Illustrations copyright © 2004 by Laura Huliska-Beith
Manufactured in China by South China Printing Company Ltd.
All rights reserved. · www.harperchildrens.com
Library of Congress Cataloging-in-Publication Data · Low, Alice.
Aunt Lucy went to buy a hat / by Alice Low ; illustrated by
Laura Huliska-Beith.— 1st ed. · p. cm.
Summary: Rhyming tale of a woman who sets out to replace her lost
hat, but winds up with a cat and a succession of other items instead.
ISBN 0-06-008971-7 – ISBN 0-06-008972-5 (lib. bdg.)
[1. Shopping—Fiction. 2. Hats—Fiction. 3. Humorous stories.
4. Stories in rhyme.] I. Huliska-Beith, Laura, ill. II. Title.
PZ8.3.L946Au 2004 · [E]—dc21 · 2003003785
Typography by Stephanie Bart-Horvath
1 2 3 4 5 6 7 8 9 10
❖
First
Edition

Aunt Lucy Went to Buy a Hat

By Alice Low

Illustrated by Laura Huliska-Beith

HarperCollinsPublishers

"My brand-new,
bright blue hat!

Drat!"

Your hat!
Your hat!

AUNT LUCY

Aunt Lucy went to buy a **hat** . . .

She really **meant**
TO buy a hat,
A hat **wide brimmed**
And trimmed with lace
TO keep the sunshine
Off her face . . .

Instead she bought a **CAT**.

Aunt Lucy went to buy
some **milk**,
Milk for the cat,
NOT for the hat,
Milk in a cup
For lapping up . . .

Instead she bought **RED SILK**.

Milk! I want milk!

Aunt Lucy went
TO buy **red thread**,
Thread for the silk,
NOT for the milk,
TO sew a gown
TO wear in town . . .

Instead she bought a **BED**.

Aunt Lucy went
To buy a **sheet**,
A sheet for the bed,
NOT for the thread,
A sheet with dots
Or tulip pots . . .

"**Hey, wait**," she said,
"I want a hat . . .
A hat wide brimmed
And trimmed with lace
To keep the sunshine
Off my face,
Not **milk** or **silk**
Or a **bed** or **thread**,
Not **tender meat**
Or a **dotted sheet**,

I WANT
A HAT!

That's that."

Then the wind went **whoosh** and it blew a hat,

And **lickety-split**,
That **zippity cat**
Ran after that hat,
up hill and down,
As it **dipped** and **flipped**
To the end of town.
That cat gave chase
Like an acrobat
Till it caught the lace
of that wide-brimmed **hat**.

"Why, look at that,
you **darling** cat!
You brought me this
Delightful hat . . .

"A hat wide brimmed
And trimmed with lace
To keep the sunshine
Off my face.
You're one **terrific** cat!"

Then she gave the ham
To a farmer man
For a jug of milk,
NOT a bolt of silk,
And the cat went

**Slurp-slurp-
lap-lap-lap . . .**

And the two collapsed
For a well-earned nap.

Now who'd imagine
All of that
From going out
To buy a hat?